Be Careful What You Wish For . . .

Hannah and Jesse found a mysterious bottle in Fear Lake. Even though it was labeled DO NOT OPEN, Jesse just had to find out what was inside.

Or, rather, *who* was inside.

Gene, the genie who pops out, grants Hannah and Jesse three wishes. All right! Hannah thinks. But Gene's been stuck in the bottle for a hundred years, and his magic's a little rusty. Will Gene make Hannah and Jesse's dreams come true? Or bring their worst nightmares to life?

Also from R. L. Stine

The Beast
The Beast 2

R. L. Stine's Ghosts of Fear Street

Available from MINSTREL Books

THREE EVIL WISHES

A Parachute Press Book

A
MINSTREL®
BOOK

Published by POCKET BOOKS
New York London Toronto Sydney Tokyo Singapore

A MINSTREL PAPERBACK *Original*

 A Minstrel Paperback published by
POCKET BOOKS, a division of Simon & Schuster Inc.
1230 Avenue of the Americas, New York, NY 10020

Copyright © 1997 by Parachute Press, Inc.

THREE EVIL WISHES WRITTEN BY CAROLYN CRIMI

ISBN: 0-671-00189-2

First Minstrel Books paperback printing April 1997

10 9 8 7 6 5 4 3 2 1

FEAR STREET is a registered trademark of Parachute Press, Inc.

A MINSTREL BOOK and colophon are registered trademarks
of Simon & Schuster Inc.

Cover art by Mark Garro

Printed in the U.S.A.

I

"**W**hy can't I get this dumb nose right?" I cried.

I always talk to myself when I'm working on my sculptures. It helps me be more creative.

But today it wasn't helping. No matter what I did, I couldn't get my life-size sculpture of Jesse right. The nose was all wrong. It made him look like a monkey.

Even though Jesse is my stepbrother, we look a bit alike. We both have pale blond hair. And we're both sort of short.

Okay, okay. We're both *really* short.

In fact, when Professor Pollack, my sculpture teacher, gave me the clay to make a life-size sculpture of myself, I had enough left over to make one of Jesse!

Last summer Mom decided I had talent in art. So she signed me up for an advanced sculpture class at Waynesbridge College. I'm twelve, so it's kind of weird going to class with college kids. At least it was weird at first. But I'm used to it now.

My mom loves everything I make. She sighs and says dopey stuff like: "Oh, Hannah, it's so wonderful to have an artist in the family." She even turned part of our garage into a studio for me.

My studio is great. It has absolutely everything I need—a sink, palette knives, and tons of paint-brushes. I even have a full-length mirror against the wall so I can paint and sculpt myself.

The only problem with my studio is that it's on Fear Street.

So is my house. Everyone knows that scary things happen on Fear Street. Kids at school tell stories all the time about ghosts and strange creatures roaming the Fear Street woods.

I've lived here all my life, and so far no creepy things have happened to me. But I'm always watching for them.

"Ark, ark-ark!!"

My dog, Barky, the smallest dog on the planet, yapped at himself in the full-length mirror. Every time Barky passes that mirror he yaps. He's cute, but he's not exactly a genius.

"Ark, ark-ark!!"

Want to guess how Barky got his name?

"Will you *please* stop it? I'm trying to work," I scolded the dog. Of course, he didn't listen.

"Ark, ark-ark!"

"What are you barking at?" I shouted at him.

I jumped as the garage door rolled open with a roar.

My stepbrother Jesse burst into the garage. "My sneakers! My sneakers!" he croaked.

I spun away from my sculpture. "Jesse, what's your problem?" I demanded.

"They . . . they got my sneakers!" he choked out, his face bright red.

I lowered my eyes to the garage floor. Jesse's sneakers were drenched in mud.

I swallowed hard. I knew what had happened. He didn't have to tell me. "The Burger brothers?" I asked softly.

Jesse nodded. "The Burger brothers."

Mike and Roy Burger are two huge walruses pretending to be twelve-year-old kids. Really. They're the biggest kids in history!

And since Jesse and I are just about the shrimp-iest kids in Shadyside, guess who the bouncing Burger brothers choose to pick on all the time?

You got it.

"They stomped mud on my new white high-tops," Jesse wailed, shaking his head. "Then Mike held me down and Roy unlaced both sneakers and took the laces."

Jesse took several deep breaths, trying to get himself together.

"Then what did they do?" I asked.

"Then they took off," he answered. "What else?"

The Burger brothers always act fast, then run away.

"Why did they do it?" I asked. Stupid question. Because I already knew the answer. They did it because they're the Burger brothers.

Jesse shrugged. "Who knows why they did it. You know Mike and Roy. They never talk. They only grunt."

Jesse is right. The longest sentence I ever heard a Burger brother say is "Yo."

Jesse sloshed around the garage in his muddy, open sneakers. "I'm *sick* of their stupid jokes. I'm *sick* of the names they call me. And I'm *sick* of those stupid skateboards they're always riding," he wailed.

"Sorry, Jesse," I replied. "There's not a lot we can do. They're big. We're small. Big kids pick on small kids. They can't help themselves. It's in their nature."

"Well, it's not fair!" Jesse scowled. Then his face brightened. "Hey!" he shouted. "Maybe if I start working out. You know, lifting weights, getting myself really pumped up. Maybe then I could take on those Burgers!"

He stepped in front of the full-length mirror. He stuck his chest out and then curled his arms up like a weight lifter does.

I burst out laughing. I couldn't help it. Jesse didn't look much like Arnold Schwarzenegger. Actually, he looked more like a little blond mouse.

"It's not funny, Hannah!" Jesse snapped. "I have to do *something*. Those big elephants think they're funny—but they're not. Last week, when they tied me to that tree—"

I shook my head slowly, remembering. Poor Jesse. The Burger brothers tied him to the tree in our neighbor's yard and left him there. It was horrible! Even worse, the tree was covered with ants!

If Barky hadn't started barking his head off, Jesse might still be out there. Luckily, I heard his yelps and came and rescued my brother.

Jesse wasn't hurt or anything. But he still has nightmares about ants crawling all over his body. And he still itches like crazy.

"I can't wear these sneakers," Jesse moaned. "Even with new laces. *Look* at them!" He paced back and forth. The sneakers made a loud sloshing sound on the concrete garage floor. "How can I get Dad to buy me new ones?"

"We'll think of something," I replied.

But I wasn't so sure. Jesse's father—my stepfather—hates to waste money. He freaks out if we leave a light on or turn the heat up even one degree. *No way* he'd pay for a new pair of sneakers after he just bought a pair.

Poor Jesse might be sloshing for weeks!

Jesse moved back in front of the mirror to flex his scrawny arms. I returned to my sculpture. Maybe now that Jesse stood in front of me, I'd be able to get the nose right.

I began to pick away at the clay—when I heard a noise outside the garage.

"Jess, what was that?" I whispered.

Jesse's arms drooped. He spun away from the mirror.

Barky perked up his ears.

This time we both heard the noise. And recognized it.

The scrape of plastic wheels on pavement.

Shoosh! Shoosh!

Skateboards!

"They're here!" Jesse cried. "Oh, no! The Burger brothers—they're here!"

6

2

*S*hoosh! *Shoosh!*

The scrape of the skateboards became a roar.

"We're trapped!" I cried. "We can't get to the house before—before—"

"Hide!" Jesse whispered. He dove behind the full-length mirror. I scrambled into the corner behind a stack of boxes and held my breath. Barky tore toward the open garage door, yapping and barking.

"No, Barky!" I whispered. *"No!"*

Too late. The little dog raced out the door. The Burger brothers had him now for sure.

"Come here, Barky! Good doggie!" I heard a tiny, shrill voice call.

"Oh, wow," I moaned, rolling my eyes.

I crawled out of my hiding place and peered outside. Just as I suspected. *Not* the Burger brothers.

Tori Sanders, the three-year-old from next door, was petting Barky in the driveway. Tori sat on one of those plastic Big Wheels. *Her* wheels made that scraping sound!

"You can come out now," I called to Jesse.

He peeked out from behind the mirror. He groaned when he saw Tori. "Well, it sounded like skateboards to me," Jesse muttered. He crawled out and dusted himself off. "But this just proves what I'm saying. It's not fair. The Burger brothers have made me scared of *everything.*"

"So what can we do?" I sighed, watching Tori pet the dog. "We're stuck with Mike and Roy. We can't *wish* them away—can we?"

After school the next afternoon, Jesse and I stopped home for Barky. Then we made our way to Fear Lake. Fear Lake is a short walk through the Fear Street woods. The woods are dark and creepy. But the lake is quiet and pretty.

When we arrived, the lakeshore was deserted. The bright afternoon sunlight glistened on the surface of the still water.

Jesse and I dropped our backpacks on the ground and began hunting for flat stones.

He and I have a championship stone-skipping contest. Until last month Jesse was the winner, with nine skips to one stone. Then I beat him with a super-flat stone that skipped ten times.

"Too round. Too round. Too round." Jesse was picking up stones and tossing them back down. "Too round. Perfect!"

I rolled my eyes. Sometimes Jesse gets way too serious about the silliest things.

I bent down to pick up a smooth white stone. Above me, the sun moved behind a thick cloud. A wave of cold rushed over me.

The lakeshore suddenly grew quieter. No branches rustled. No leaves whispered in the trees.

Jesse didn't seem to notice.

I stood up and gazed around.

Yes. It had definitely grown quieter. Another chill ran down my back. The same chill I feel when I think someone's watching me.

Barky started yapping. "ARK, ARK, ARK!!"

"Barky, be quiet!" Jesse ordered.

Barky ran clockwise in little circles, barking furiously. Then he ran counterclockwise, barking and staring into the woods the whole time.

"What is his problem?" I cried. "What does he see?"

I tried to follow Barky's stare.

The low shrubs suddenly shook. A branch cracked on the ground.

It must be some kind of creature! I realized.

Barky has sniffed out a creature from the woods back there.

My eyes narrowed on the cluster of leafy shrubs.

The shrubs shook again.

Then a dark form moved out from behind them.

And I started to scream.

3

"No," I cried. "It can't be!"

A second form stepped out from the bushes.

The Burger brothers.

No wonder Barky was yapping his head off!

"Yo!" Mike called.

"Hey—yo!" Roy greeted us.

"Wow! Two words! Good vocabulary!" Jesse exclaimed.

I shoved him. "Shut up! Don't get them angry."

The Burger brothers shuffled toward us. Their big bellies bounced under their T-shirts. Their dirty brown hair was combed over their foreheads, nearly covering their puffy, round blue eyes.

"What are you doing here? Leave us alone!" I snapped.

Mike grunted.

Roy muttered something I couldn't hear.

Barky yapped angrily at them.

"You're scaring our dog!" Jesse cried.

Roy snickered.

"That's a dog?" Mike asked. "Sure it isn't a rat? Huh-huh-huh."

"That's not a rat," Roy added. "It's a gerbil."

They both held their big stomachs and laughed really loud. Big, fake laughs.

Barky growled.

"Kind of ugly for a gerbil," Roy said, eyeing Barky.

"That dog looks like something I picked out of my nose," Mike declared.

They laughed again.

I noticed Jesse picking up a stone. A pretty big stone. He hid it in his fist.

Oh, no, I thought. Don't start trouble, Jesse. Don't try to act brave with these two guys.

Mike turned to me. "Yo. How come you're here?"

"We're . . . skipping stones," I told him.

He scratched his thick brown hair. His round eyes grew wider. "Yeah?"

"Hey—show us how," his brother demanded.

"Yeah," Mike agreed.

"No problem," I said. I picked up a flat white stone. Then I stepped to the edge of the shore. Pulled my hand back. And tossed the stone across the surface of the lake.

It skipped twice before it sank.

"You stink," Roy told me.

Mike let out a high-pitched giggle. He shoved Jesse toward the water. "You try, shrimp."

"Okay, okay," Jesse muttered. He already had the stone in his hand. He heaved it hard. It skipped once, then it sank into the blue-green water.

"You stink too," Roy observed.

Jesse turned on him angrily. "Can you do better?" he demanded.

"Yeah. Watch," Roy replied.

He picked up Jesse's backpack. Raised it high above his head.

And heaved it into the lake.

"Hey!" Jesse shrieked.

The black backpack floated on top of the water for about five seconds. Then it sank to the bottom.

"Wow," Roy muttered, staring at the water. A wicked grin spread across his face. "It didn't skip."

"Let *me* try!" Mike declared.

He picked up my backpack and tossed it into the water. It sank even quicker than Jesse's.

"Mine didn't skip either," Mike said, pretending to pout.

"Guess you two win!" Roy exclaimed.

The two of them bounced off into the woods, laughing their blubbery heads off.

Jesse and I stared at the lake. My mouth dropped open. My legs suddenly felt rubbery and weak.

Our books. Our homework. All on the bottom of Fear Lake.

"I'm going to get them one day!" Jesse's voice was low and angry. He balled his hands into fists. "My science project is in my backpack. My homework is in there. My textbooks. Everything!"

We stared at the water in silence.

"At least they didn't throw them very far," I said finally. "Maybe we can pull them up and dry our stuff out."

Jesse stared at me. "You really want to go in *there? In Fear Lake?*"

The lake, just like the woods, had a pretty creepy reputation. "No. I don't *want* to go in," I replied. "But what choice do we have?"

Jesse knew we *had* no choice. We had to go in.

We pulled off our shoes and socks and rolled up our jeans as high as they would go.

"That water is going to be freezing," Jesse warned.

I hoped he was wrong. I walked up to the edge of the lake and peered in. Above, the sun slid behind clouds again. The water was so dark and cloudy, I could barely see the bottom. I dipped my big toe in for half a second—and drew it back.

Cold. Very cold.

"I can't believe the Burger brothers did this to us!" I cried. "I *wish* we could pay them back!"

I took a deep breath and waded into the cold water, moving as fast as I could. The cold took my breath away. I gasped. And shivered. And gasped again. I wrapped my arms around my body to keep warm.

"Whooooa!" I shouted. Did something slimy brush up against my leg? It sure felt like it. And in Fear Lake, I wasn't taking any chances. I started to wade back to the shore—fast.

"Jesse! Something's here—in the water!" I shouted. "Something *alive!*"

Jesse grabbed my wrist. "Yeah. They're called *fish.*"

Together we walked a few more steps into the dark, cold water. Then, in front of me, something splashed to the surface.

A fish?

No. It bobbed in slow circles just under the surface.

What could it be?

"Got it!" Jesse cried.

He yanked his backpack up from the water. "Yuuuck!" he moaned. The backpack was covered in black mud.

I lowered my eyes to the water. The strange object began to bob toward me!

A voice in the back of my mind told me to get out of the lake right away. To stay away from that thing in the water.

I should have listened.

But instead, I took a step forward. I squeezed my eyes shut—and reached out to grab it.

4

I wrapped my fingers around the object. It felt slick and hard. I pulled it out of the water and held it up to examine it.

A bottle?

Yes. It *was* a bottle. An ordinary brown glass bottle with a cork in it.

I let out a sigh of relief. Nothing spooky or weird about a bottle. Someone probably threw it in the lake after a picnic.

I was about to drop the bottle back into the water, when I noticed something strange about it. It should have been cold—but it felt warm. Warmer than my hand.

I held on to the bottle as I hunted for my backpack.

"Found it," I called to Jesse, who was already onshore.

I dredged up my backpack. Gross. It was muddy and covered with clumps of soggy green weeds.

I waded back to shore with the bottle and my backpack. "Hey, Jess. Check out this bottle. It feels warm and—"

The bottle jerked in my hand!

I nearly dropped it.

Did something *move* inside it? Was something *alive* in there?

I tried to peer through the brown glass. But it was thick and dirty. I couldn't see a thing.

Get a grip, Hannah! I thought to myself. Nothing could be living in this old bottle.

I turned to Jesse. He frowned as he stared at his mud-soaked backpack. "Totally ruined," he moaned, shaking his head. "Now I have to tell Dad about my sneakers *and* my backpack. He'll freak. He'll totally freak."

I began to answer Jesse, when I felt my hand grow warmer. The bottle was heating up! It jerked in my hand again. Harder this time.

Something very weird was going on here. I set the bottle down in the grass. I didn't want to hold on to it another second.

"Hey, what's that?" Jesse asked, nodding his head toward the bottle.

"What does it look like, brain? It's a bottle I found in the lake."

"Wow. It looks *really* old," he said, bending down to examine it.

He reached out and picked it up. "Yuck! It's . . . it's *hot!*"

So I wasn't going crazy! There really *was* something strange about that bottle.

Jesse held it up to the sun. He squinted his eyes, trying to peer inside.

"Is there a note inside? People always do that in the movies."

"I found this in the *lake,* Jesse. People don't throw bottles with notes in them in a lake. They throw them in the ocean to see how far they will travel."

"Hey, maybe it's got money inside!" Jesse cried. He tried even harder to see through the dark brown glass. He shook the bottle.

"Oh, yeah, people are *always* throwing bottles filled with money into the lake." I scowled at my brother. "Look, just put it down, okay? We're soaked. We have to go home and change."

Jesse ignored me as he squinted at the bottle. "Hey, it feels as if it's getting even warmer."

"Jess, put it down!" I insisted. My voice quivered.

"What's your problem, Hannah? It's just a bottle." He turned it around in his hand, inspecting every inch. "I'm going to open it."

"No! Wait!" I cried. I grabbed the bottle from him. "There's something written on the side. Maybe it's important."

"If you say so." Jesse sighed.

A yellow label clung to the side of the bottle. The letters on it were so faded, I could barely make them out.

" 'Danger,' " I read out loud. " 'Do not open.' "

The bottle began to vibrate in my hand.

I jumped.

This was definitely *not* my imagination.

I dropped the bottle back to the ground and kicked it away. "This bottle is bad news. I'm not opening it! I don't even want it near me!"

It sat there on its side in the grass. Then, slowly, it rolled back to me.

"Did you see that, Jesse?" I whispered. "It—it moved on its own!"

Jesse groaned and picked up the bottle again. "It just rolled. Bottles do that."

"Let's go," I urged. "I told you what it says on the label. We are *not* supposed to open this bottle."

Jesse took hold of the cork. "That's stupid."

"No, Jesse, *don't!*"

I reached out to swipe the bottle from him.

Too late.

He grasped the cork and tugged it out of the bottle.

5

The cork came away from the bottle with a loud *pop!* And a stream of thick purple gas shot out of the opening.

Ohhhh! What a *sick* smell!

I started to choke on the sour gas. I held my breath and clutched my throat with my hands.

Jesse was sputtering and coughing. The bottle thudded onto the ground as it fell from Jesse's hand.

The awful purple gas swirled around us like a tornado. It lifted up leaves and twigs. It howled through the trees.

"Wh-what's going on?" Jesse choked out.

I dropped to my knees and grabbed for the bottle.

I thought maybe I could cork it back up. Stop the gas from shooting out.

I gripped the bottle in one hand. But where was the cork?

Before I had a chance to search, I heard my brother's cry.

"Hannah—whooooa! Check it out!"

I raised my eyes. Dark purple clouds of smoke gathered together, growing thicker.

"Jesse, *what's happening?*" I shouted above the roar of the swirling wind.

The purple clouds floated together to form a thick ball of whirling gas. I crouched down close to the ground and held my breath. I squinted as the howling wind whipped dirt and leaves into my face.

The purple clouds pulled together. Thickened. Took shape.

I saw two arms. A broad chest. Two legs formed from the swirling purple gas.

The purple clouds tossed and tumbled.

And then a head rose on top of the swirling body. A man's head. An old man's head.

The smoke stopped twirling. The body settled to the ground.

The howl of the wind ended. All was silent now.

No more swirling gusts of gas. Only the sour smell remained.

Jesse and I gaped in amazement. The old man—

all purple, all shades of purple—stood before us in a flowing purple robe. He blinked his purple eyes. He worked his jaw and rubbed his chin.

"Who—who *are* you?" I choked out. My whole body was shaking. I hugged myself to stop the trembling.

Barky growled and hid behind me.

The purple man raised one arm high in the air.

I gasped. What did he plan to do?

He turned his head slowly—and sniffed his armpit!

"Whew!" He made a disgusted face and turned to me.

"You'd stink too if you'd been inside a bottle for a hundred years!" he cried. He had a raspy, old man's voice. He held his nose. "Hoo. I need a bath. A *long* bath!"

With a groan, he raised both arms high above his head. Then he stretched his arms, his legs, his back. "Hoo. That feels good." He smiled. "I need a massage. That's what I need. Being folded up so small gives me such a cramp!"

Jesse still hadn't closed his mouth. He gaped at the purple man in shock. "Are you for real?" my brother blurted out.

The old man continued stretching. Rubbing the back of his neck. He gazed down at my brother. "Who's to say what's real and what isn't real?"

"But did you really come out of that bottle?" Jesse demanded.

"I didn't take a taxi!" the old man replied.

Despite my fear, I chuckled. The old guy was funny.

He stopped stretching and made a short bow to us. "I'd bow lower," he told us. "But my back is killing me."

"Why are you bowing to us?" I asked.

"You are my new masters," he replied. He studied Jesse, then me. "How come you're so short?"

"Give us a break!" I cried.

"We're still growing," Jesse added.

"You're *children?*" The old man slapped his forehead. *"This* is what children look like these days?"

He narrowed his eyes at me. "Young lady, how can you walk in the woods without a bonnet?"

"I don't own any bonnets," I replied. "I wouldn't even know where to buy one."

He rubbed his chin. "Hoo. I've got a lot to learn." He sniffed his armpit again. "I'm stinking up the joint. I apologize."

"Who—who *are* you?" I stammered.

He cleared his throat. "Allow me to introduce myself. My name is All-Powerful Magical Genie of the Lost Kingdoms of the Great and Golden Raj."

"Whoa. That's a long name!" I cried.

"Most people call me Gene," he replied.

"You're a *genie?* A real live *genie?* No way!" Jesse exclaimed.

"It's a living," Gene muttered with a shrug. "Keeps me out of trouble."

I gazed up at him. "You're a genie? Just like in all the old stories?"

He nodded. "Well . . . in the stories the genies don't have heartburn the way I do!" He pounded his chest. "Hoo. I need some seltzer. You build up a thirst bobbing around in a bottle. Take my word."

His expression changed. His purple eyes had been twinkling. Now they darkened.

"I can grant you three wishes," he said solemnly.

"Just like in the old stories!" Jesse cried.

"Could you please stop saying that?" Gene groaned. "I'm not as *old* as I look."

"Sorry," Jesse murmured.

"Now, as I was saying, you get three wishes. Anything you want. You name it—it's yours!" Gene paused and smiled, showing two rows of crooked purple teeth.

"But beware," he continued. "Once you've made your three wishes, that's it! No more! They're gone for good! And you cannot reverse them—so don't even ask."

Jesse and I exchanged glances. "Oh, wow! This is

26

so cool!" Jesse cried. "Let's do it, Hannah! Let's make a wish right now!"

A cold feeling swept down my back. "I—I don't know," I stuttered. "Wishes don't always work out in those old stories."

The old genie shrugged. "It's up to you. You take a chance. Or you don't take a chance."

"I want to take a chance," Jesse insisted. "Let's see . . . I wish—"

"Jesse!" I clamped a hand over my brother's mouth. And pulled him toward the lake. "Think about this," I whispered. "I found the bottle in *Fear Lake*. Nothing but evil ever comes out of there. If *he* came out of Fear Lake, *he's* probably evil too."

"I know I can talk her into this," Jesse called to Gene over my shoulder. "If you'll just give us a few minutes."

"Take your time," the old man rasped. "I have been waiting for someone to open my bottle for one hundred years. I'm enjoying the fresh air."

He took a deep breath. "Hope my allergies don't act up. I started sneezing inside the bottle. Nearly blew my brains out!"

Jesse took my arm and led me to the shore. "Come on, Hannah. Stop being such a chicken. Let's make a wish," he urged. "Just think of all the cool things we can wish for! How can we pass it up?"

27

"You're not thinking clearly," I told him. "You're not thinking about the *bad* things that could happen. This could be really dangerous, Jesse. How do we know we can trust the old guy? How?"

"Hannah, we're the *masters* here," Jesse insisted. "He said we were his masters. That means he can't do anything unless we tell him to. What could possibly go wrong?"

Jesse had a point. Gene did say we were the masters.

I stole a glance at Gene. He was taking deep breaths. Coughing. Stretching his arms. He smiled at me. A strange smile.

No. We shouldn't be messing with this guy, I thought. Something bad would happen. I just felt it.

Then I thought again of what Jesse said. We could wish for anything we wanted. *Anything!*

I gazed at the genie. Then I gazed at Jesse.

Should we make a wish?

Should we?

6

Why not? I decided. "Okay, Jesse. Let's try it."

"Yes!" Jesse cried. He pumped his fist in the air.

Gene rubbed his hands together. "Good choice," he said. "That's the choice I would have made."

My stomach tightened with excitement. I began to think of what I could wish for. My eyes wandered around the lake. They came to rest on our mud-soaked backpacks.

An idea began to take shape in my mind.

A great idea.

An idea I knew Jesse would love.

"I've got it," I told Jesse. "I know what we should wish for."

Jesse studied me, interested. "Yeah? What?"

"What if we could get revenge on the Burger brothers?" I suggested.

Jesse's face lit up. "All right! That would be awesome! But how?"

I whispered my idea into Jesse's ear.

"Secrets?" the old genie cried. "If you want your wish, you can't keep it a secret. Genies really don't like secrets."

I started to reply. But a sudden gurgling sound behind me made me turn to the lake.

Bubbles rose onto the surface of the lake. Wisps of steam started to lift off the water.

The water churned and foamed.

I gasped when I realized the lake was boiling!

"Are *you* doing that?" I asked the genie.

He nodded. "I do not like whispering!"

"Okay, okay! We're sorry!" Jesse cried. "We won't whisper anymore!"

Gene's face relaxed. "Impressive trick, huh? Actually, it's as easy as boiling water."

The water calmed. The steam vanished.

"That was too cool!" Jesse declared.

But my stomach tightened even more. "We'd better be careful not to get on his bad side," I warned Jesse. "What if he decided to boil *us?*"

"Hoo. I'm getting too much sun," Gene complained. "You know, I've been in the shade for a hundred years. I'm not used to all this sunlight. Got a wish yet?"

I straightened up. I cleared my throat. "I wish

that Jesse and I were bigger and stronger than Mike and Roy Burger!" I announced.

I glanced at Jesse. He nodded his head in agreement.

Gene bowed to us again. "Your wish is my command," he said solemnly.

The genie closed his eyes and let his chin drop to his chest. Then he raised his arms up to the sky and waved them from side to side. He swung his hips back and forth.

I stifled a giggle. Gene appeared to be doing some strange sort of hula dance!

A rumble—like thunder—rolled over the sky.

I gazed up.

And saw a swirling mass of purple smoke spinning downward.

Coming right at us.

"Get down!" I ordered Jesse. I grabbed him and pulled him to the ground.

The tornado of purple gas swept over us. It whipped twigs and leaves into our faces.

A heavy branch splintered off a tree. It slammed the ground as it fell. Landed a few inches from us.

The purple tornado swept around us, blinding us. I couldn't breathe!

This was a big mistake, I thought, my whole body shaking. *A really big mistake.*

"Jesse, where are you?" I shouted. "I can't see you!"

No answer.

"Jesse!" I shouted.

The disgusting purple gas covered me. My skin started to prickle, as if someone were jabbing hundreds of needles into it.

I rubbed my arms frantically, trying to make it stop itching.

"What's happening? What's happening to me?" I screamed.

From somewhere far, far away, I could hear Barky yapping excitedly.

Pain shot through my arms and legs. I could feel my muscles and bones shifting and stretching. My skin tightened, as if it were going to rip right off my body.

"Noooo!" A horrified wail escaped my throat.

I heard a loud ripping sound.

I gasped for breath as the purple smoke cleared.

Frantically, I examined myself. That ripping sound—it was my clothes. My jeans—my shirt—were ripped to shreds!

I was alive. I was okay.

But somehow I felt different.

Really different.

What had happened? I gazed around, searching for Jesse.

And screamed.

7

"**O**h, no! *Nooooo!*"

I stared down at Jesse. He hadn't changed a bit. But me?

"I—I'm a *giant!*" I shrieked. I turned to the genie. "What have you done to me?"

I was enormous! At least eight feet tall and as wide as a garage!

I stared down at my huge body in horror. Big muscles bulged all over me. Huge, rippling muscles like a bodybuilder's.

"Hannah? What happened?" Jesse cried in a tiny voice. "You changed—but I didn't!"

"How come Jesse is the same size?" I bellowed at the genie. My big voice boomed through the woods.

"Wow! You could handle the Burger brothers now—easy!" Jesse exclaimed. He laughed.

"Shut up! It's not funny!" I bellowed at him. "You'd better not laugh!"

That made Jesse laugh harder.

"If you don't stop laughing I'll . . . I'll sit on you!" I cried.

That shut him up.

I rubbed my neck. It was so thick, I couldn't even get my fingers around it. As thick as a tree trunk. I felt too heavy to move. Too heavy to breathe.

All this while, the purple genie hadn't said a word. Now I stepped toward him angrily, my big fists churning the air. "What happened?" I demanded. "You turned me into a muscle-bound giant. And—and—"

Before he could reply, a loud roar burst into my ears.

I whipped around—as a ferocious, snarling animal leapt onto my chest!

8

I toppled backward onto the grass.

"Ooof!" I landed hard on my back. Nearly knocked my breath out.

No time to scramble away.

The big creature pounced.

It jumped on top of me. Its heavy paws thudded onto my chest.

Pinned me to the ground.

Another roar burst from its open jaws.

I shot up my hands. Struggled to push it away.

Its hot breath swept over my face. Its pointed teeth gleamed above me.

"Hellllp!"

My cry was smothered as the beast lowered its enormous head—and licked my nose!

"Barky—get off!" I shrieked.

The giant dog licked my cheeks and forehead.

"Barky! Off!"

I pushed the excited dog away and scrambled to my feet.

Jesse had backed up to the trunk of a willow tree. His eyes were wide with amazement. "Barky is a giant too?" he choked out.

"Sit, Barky! Sit!" I commanded.

The big dog obediently sat down, but his enormous tail continued to wag, sending up clouds of dust.

I turned angrily to the genie. "You messed up!" I shrieked.

His purple face darkened. He glanced away.

"Look at me! Look at Barky! You messed up!" I wailed.

He shrugged. "Must be my eyesight," he murmured, still avoiding my stare. "You know. A hundred years of staring out through a brown bottle."

"But—but—but—" I sputtered.

"I thought I was changing you and your brother," Gene continued. "I didn't see the pooch standing there."

That made me totally lose it. "But *look what you did to me!*" I shrieked. "I'm a freak! A giant, muscle-bound freak!"

He rubbed his chin. "You said you wanted to be bigger and stronger than some other kids. So I made you bigger and stronger."

I opened my mouth to speak. But no sound came out.

I was too furious to speak!

I stared at Barky—nearly as big as a horse. And then my eyes moved to my tiny little shrimp of a brother.

I waved my fist in the air. Big muscles rippled up and down my arm.

"Change me back," I told the genie. "I mean it. Change Barky and me back the way we were."

"I'm sorry," he said softly, eyes lowered to the ground. "I can't."

9

"You can't?" I cried. "What do you mean, you *can't?*"

"Okay. Okay," Gene said, motioning for me to calm down. "Stop shouting. Hoo. You're giving me a splitting headache."

"Change Barky and me back!" I insisted.

"All right," he finally agreed. "I can change you back. But it will cost you a wish."

"Excuse me? No way!" Jesse protested. "You're the one who messed up! Why should *we* waste a wish because you made a mistake?"

The genie stuck out his purple chin. "Those are the rules, kids. Want to change back? It costs a wish. I don't write the rules. I only carry them out. It's a job, you know."

"A real genie would admit that he was wrong," I grumbled. "A *real* genie would change us back for free. I guess you're just a big fake—with a capital F."

The genie's purple eyes flashed with anger. "You shouldn't call me names," he scolded. "I'm trying to teach you a few things here. You shouldn't whisper, and you shouldn't call names."

A wave of hot air swirled around me. Choking me. I gasped for breath. Behind me I heard the lake water bubble and churn again.

I felt weak and dizzy. Sweat poured down my face. "Okay! I'm sorry!" I cried. "You're *not* a fake!"

The genie waved a hand, and the waves of heat disappeared.

A cool breeze brushed against my skin. I took a deep breath and let the fresh air wash over me.

"You okay, Hannah?" Jesse asked.

"Yeah, I think so," I told him.

That settled it. Now I *knew* we had to stay on Gene's good side. He was powerful. Very powerful. And he could use that power against us even if he said we were the masters.

"I have decided to give you a break," Gene said finally. "I admit there was a tiny mix-up. So I'll change you and the dog back. But next time you'll have to use a wish!"

Gene bowed to Barky and me. Then he closed his eyes and started to hum. He tilted his face up to the sky and waved his arms in the air. He began to dance his crazy hula.

I held on tight to Barky as the tornado of swirling purple gas blasted out of the sky and covered us both again. The prickling sensation spread over my skin.

Barky yapped furiously. I held him in place with my huge arms.

As I struggled to keep Barky close to me, I had a terrible thought. What if Gene messes up again? What if he makes me *too* small this time? Or even bigger?

I buried my face in Barky's fur. Get it right this time, Gene, I pleaded silently.

The purple smoke cleared as quickly as it appeared. I glanced down at my feet. They appeared normal again. I felt my neck.

Yes! As scrawny as ever.

I turned to Barky. He barked and wagged his tiny tail.

He was back to normal too.

I sighed and stretched my arms above my head. It felt good to be back in my own body.

I turned to my brother. "I don't know about you,

Jesse, but I've had enough of this wish stuff for one day."

"Yeah. Me too," Jesse agreed. He dusted off his jeans and picked up his soaking-wet backpack.

"Come on, Gene. Back inside the bottle." I picked up the bottle and held it out to him. "Jump back in. We'll bring you out again later—after we have some time to think about our next wish."

Gene folded his arms across his chest. "Sorry." He shook his head.

"What do you mean?" I demanded. "We're the masters, right? What we say goes, remember?"

But Gene didn't budge. "I am *not* going back in that bottle," he argued. "I have such a pain in my neck. And my knees still ache. No way I'm going back in that cramped little bottle. You will have to take me home with you."

"Huh? You can't come home with us!" Jesse cried. "Our parents would freak!"

I poked Jesse in the ribs with my elbow. "Don't make him angry," I whispered. "We don't need any more of his hot air."

I cleared my throat and turned to Gene. "What Jesse means is that you would be kind of tough to explain to our parents. You see, we don't often meet *genies.*"

"We *never* meet genies," Jesse backed me up. "So you'll just have to get back in the bottle."

41

"Are you deaf?" the old genie rasped. "Maybe your second wish should be for a hearing aid. I am going to live outside my bottle—with you—until you have made all of your wishes."

"But my parents—" I started to say.

He raised a hand to silence me. "Don't worry about it. I've got a few tricks up my sleeve," he said. "Watch."

The old genie closed his eyes. A wisp of purple smoke rose up around him.

Panic made me cry out. What did he plan to do? Something horrible?

I squeezed my eyes shut. "No! Don't!" I yelled.

But there was no heat. No boiling lake. I opened one eye. Then the other.

Gene had disappeared. A boy our age stood in his place. A stocky boy with blue eyes and curly brown hair. He wore black velvet shorts, a ruffled shirt, and shoes that buttoned on the side.

"Gene? Is that you?" I cried.

He nodded. "Hoo. Is this a thrill? Now I'm a kid again! My heart is going pitty-pat. I may dance a jig."

"Whoa! That's awesome," Jesse shouted. "But, Gene, what are you wearing? You look like—a *girl.*"

Gene fluffed the ruffle on his shirt. "I do *not* look like a girl. These clothes are very fashionable," he insisted.

"Maybe a hundred years ago," I told him, shaking my head. "Gene, this is never going to work."

"It must work," he replied. "It is the only way you will receive the rest of your wishes."

Jesse shrugged and carefully picked up his muddy backpack. "I guess he's right. It'll have to work," he told me.

"Have you lost your mind? What are we going to tell Mom and Dad?" I asked.

Jesse slipped the bottle into my backpack and then handed the pack to me. "We'll think of something," he said cheerfully. "Besides, we have two wishes left! We can't just forget about them!"

"Yeah, well, the first wish didn't turn out so great," I reminded him.

"So we'll be a little more careful next time. We'll get our wishes, and then—poof!—Gene will be on his way. Right, Gene?"

"Whatever," the genie muttered. "If I'm a kid, how come I've still got such heartburn?"

"Well . . . all right," I gave in. "I guess Gene can come with us."

But as we made our way home, my mind filled with dread.

How could we just bring a new kid home to live?

How could we ever explain this to Mom and Dad?

And what if the genie wasn't as nice as he seemed?

What if this was some kind of trick? What if he really was evil?

10

"This is Gene," I told my parents.

Gene gave them a little bow.

We made Gene change into modern clothes before we reached the house. He looked pretty good. But his skin was still a little purple. I hoped my parents wouldn't notice.

"How are you, Gene?" Dad shook his hand.

"Actually, I've got pretty bad heartburn," Gene complained, pounding his chest. "Hoo. Have I got heartburn."

"Heartburn?" Dad narrowed his eyes at our guest. "A boy your age?"

"Have you got any seltzer?" Gene asked. "I've really got to burp. I think it will help a lot."

His eyes were flashing around the kitchen. I knew he was admiring all the fancy new appliances. After all, he hadn't been in a kitchen in a hundred years.

Dad shook his head. He reached into the fridge for some club soda. "Weird friend," he whispered to me.

"He's Jesse's friend," I whispered back. "Not mine."

Gene gulped down the club soda in a single swallow. A few seconds later he was burping his head off. It was really gross.

I thought there was no way my parents would let Gene stay for dinner. But they did. Jesse and I have really nice parents.

"We're only having pizza," Mom told me. "You've got about half an hour."

Jesse and I led Gene up to Jesse's room. "Houses have changed," Gene murmured. "No butter churn."

I turned to him. "Will you *try* to be more normal?" I whispered. "You don't want my parents to think that you're weird, do you?"

"Weird? *Me*—weird?" he replied, his eyes wide with shock. "I'm the most normal genie in the Lost Kingdoms of the Great and Golden Raj!"

"Well, try to act like a normal twelve-year-old *person,*" I pleaded.

"There's no such thing," he muttered. He picked up the remote clicker to Jesse's TV. "What's this?"

"For the TV," I explained.

"Don't spell your words out," he scolded. "Don't whisper, don't call names, and don't spell out your words! It drives me crazy!"

I pointed across the room. "That's called a *TV*," I said. "You can watch things on it."

"Here. I'll show you," Jesse offered. He took the remote clicker and turned on the TV.

Gene smiled as the picture appeared. A Bugs Bunny cartoon.

"You watch for a while," Jesse told him. He shoved me toward the door. "Hannah and I will go talk about our next wish. Okay?"

"This TV is some kind of magic," Gene said, staring at Elmer Fudd. "How does it work?"

Jesse and I closed the bedroom door behind us and made our way to the end of the hall to talk in private.

"What are we going to do?" Jesse whispered. "We have to get him out of here. He's too weird. Mom and Dad will never believe he's a normal kid."

I nodded. "I know. But how can we get rid of him?"

"Maybe we should make two more wishes—real quick," Jesse suggested. "We could—"

"Too dangerous," I interrupted. "We have to be careful. Our first wish was a disaster."

"But we know we want to do something about the Burger brothers—right?" Jesse insisted.

I shook my head. "I'm not so sure. It's all too dangerous. And Gene is *so* weird. He might mess up again and do something terrible to us."

Jesse gazed over my shoulder at the bedroom door. "It's very quiet in there," he whispered. "I don't hear the TV anymore."

"Maybe we should make two *dumb* wishes," I suggested. "You know—ask for a closet full of candy bars and a stack of hundred-dollar bills. Just to get rid of him."

"No way," Jesse replied sharply. "I just keep picturing my backpack, all soaked and drenched in mud. My science project that I worked six weeks on—totally ruined."

Jesse sighed. "I really want to pay back Mike and Roy. I really do."

"I think it's a bad idea," I insisted. "I don't think we can trust Gene. I think we have to get rid of him as fast as we can."

"Dinner!" Mom's call from downstairs interrupted our discussion.

"We'll be right down!" I called back.

Jesse and I hurried back to Jesse's room to get Gene. "Do you think he'll be okay at dinner?" I whispered.

But Jesse had no chance to answer.

We pushed open the bedroom door—and both of us gasped in horror.

First I saw bolts and wires and sheets of metal strewn over the bedroom carpet. Then I saw the TV's picture tube lying on its side in front of the dresser.

Knobs and electronic parts and circuit boards were piled beside the bed. The cable box had been taken apart. Pieces of it rested at the foot of the bed.

Gene had his back to us. He was busily pulling the speaker from what was left of the TV.

"I—I don't *believe* it!" Jesse croaked.

"Gene—what are you *doing?*" I shrieked. "You took apart the whole TV!"

He lowered the speaker to the floor. Then he

turned to us. "Just trying to figure out how it works," he replied with a grin. He shook his head. "Hoo. So many parts."

"But—but—but—" my brother sputtered.

"Don't worry," Gene assured him. "I'm pretty sure I can get it back together." He scratched his head. "Pretty sure," he muttered.

"Dinner!" Mom called from downstairs.

"My TV!" Jesse wailed. "I've had it for only a few weeks!"

"What does this do?" Gene asked. He held up a long metal tube.

"How should I know?" Jesse snapped furiously.

"Genies are very curious," Gene said, studying the tube. "You need to be curious to be a genie. If you aren't curious, you'll never learn anything— right?"

Jesse grabbed Gene by the shoulders and tugged him away from the TV. "You're not supposed to be a genie now, remember? You're supposed to be a friend who's staying for dinner."

"Do you think you can act normal?" I asked the genie. "Don't give Mom and Dad any reason to think you're weird—okay?"

"Hoo. That's easy," Gene replied, following us out of the room. "I do know how to eat. It won't be any problem."

I felt so nervous as we entered the dining room.

51

We usually eat in the kitchen. But since we had a guest, Gene, Mom and Dad set the table in the dining room.

Gene sat between Jesse and me on one side of the table. Mom and Dad were at the ends.

I had a sudden urge to blurt out the truth: "Gene isn't a kid. He's really a genie. He's been inside a bottle for a hundred years. Jesse and I pulled him out, and he's giving us three wishes."

But I knew Mom and Dad wouldn't believe me. They'd think it was some kind of dumb joke.

So I didn't say anything.

Instead, I tried to fight down my nervousness. And I silently prayed that Gene wouldn't do anything weird or embarrassing.

"Hannah, pass the pizza to Gene first," Dad instructed. He took a deep breath, inhaling the pizza aroma. "Mmmm. It looks great. Plenty of pepperoni. I don't know about you guys, but I'm starving!"

I picked up the pizza tray by the edges and held it out to Gene.

"Thank you very much," he said politely. "It does look really good."

Then he reached both hands to the tray.

He rolled the entire pizza up.

And slid the whole thing into his mouth.

* * *

After dinner I hurried out to my studio in the garage. I had to get out of the house. Away from that crazy genie.

Poor Mom and Dad.

They didn't know what to say when Gene ate the whole pizza.

They had stared at him in amazement for the longest time. Then Mom went into the kitchen, opened a can of tuna fish, and made sandwiches for the rest of us.

Gene smiled and talked about his heartburn, and acted as if he hadn't done anything wrong. Mom and Dad kept flashing me glances like "What is this kid's problem?" I could see that Dad was really angry.

Jesse hurried Gene upstairs. And I ran out to my studio. Barky followed me. I got to work on my self-portrait. I hoped that working with clay would help me feel better about Gene and wishes and pizza!

I carved away at the chin, making it a little pointier. Then I worked on the hair, the nose, and the hands. Before I knew it, an hour had gone by.

"Oh, boy, Barky, I've been working a long time." I yawned and stretched.

Barky turned toward the open garage door. He growled a low, angry growl.

"What's up, boy?" I asked.

That's when I heard it. The scraping sound of skateboard wheels.

Get a grip, Hannah, I thought. It's probably just Tori on her Big Wheels again.

But Tori wouldn't be out this late—would she?

"Ark! Ark! Ark!" my dog yapped.

My heart began thumping in my chest.

"Ark! Ark! Ark!"

I took a deep breath and went back to my work. I hoped that maybe, if I just concentrated on my sculpture, they would go away.

I wasn't that lucky.

"Hey—yo!" Mike Burger hopped off his skateboard and burst into the garage.

"Yo—hey!" His brother Roy did the same.

A chill ran up my spine. The clay fell out of my hand.

"What are you two creeps doing here? Isn't it past your bedtime?" I snapped.

"Yo. What's up?" Mike asked.

Roy stepped up to my sculpture of myself. "Who's this?" he grunted. "Your dog?"

"No way. That's a pig!" Mike declared.

They both tossed back their pudgy, round heads and giggled like hyenas. "Huh-huh-huh-huh."

"Ha-ha. Remind me to laugh," I muttered. "Would you two please leave? I'm trying to work and—*hey!*"

54

I cried out as Roy pulled the head off my sculpture. "Mike—think fast!" He heaved it across the garage to his brother.

"Stop it! Give it back!" I screamed.

I jumped up and dove at Mike. He held it up high, out of my reach.

"What do you think, Roy—dog or pig?" Mike asked his brother.

He tossed the head back to Roy.

"Monkey," Roy replied, catching the head against his chest.

"Hey, yeah," Mike agreed. "Just like this monkey in the middle!"

They tossed the head back and forth to each other. I ran between them, reaching up to catch the head—and missing. Barky ran furiously back and forth too, barking his head off.

Each time one of the Burgers caught the head, the wet clay made a sickening *splat*. And I could see the head squish flatter and flatter.

"Please stop!" I begged. "You don't know how long I worked on that!"

Roy grinned. "Okay. You can have it back. *Catch!*"

He flung the head straight up in the air.

I watched it sail up until it hit the ceiling of the garage. It stuck for a moment. Then started to fall.

I made a diving catch.

The head brushed against my fingertips. Then it splattered on the concrete floor at my feet.

I knelt by the head of my sculpture.

I picked it up. A gray, shapeless blob.

My face turned red hot. My whole body trembled with anger.

"Nice try, butterfingers," Roy giggled.

"Looks *better* to me," Mike chimed in. "I think we fixed it!"

They hooted and howled.

Then they climbed back on their skateboards and disappeared.

Okay, Burgers, I thought. You asked for it. This time you messed with me once too often.

It's payback time.

12

I found Jesse and Gene in Jesse's room. Gene was down on his hands and knees, puzzling over the pieces of the TV set.

I dragged Jesse to my room and told him that I agreed with him. "We have to make a wish to pay back the Burger brothers. But how should we ask it? We have to be careful."

"Let's just turn them into bugs or something," Jesse suggested.

I shook my head. "They already *are* bugs!" I grumbled.

I thought for a moment. "How about if we wish that they get stuck to their skateboards permanently!"

Jesse shook his head. "Not good," he murmured. "They'd probably *like* that!"

"You're right," I agreed. I rubbed the palms of my hands together, thinking. "What if we made them really fat? So fat they could barely move?"

Jesse made a face. "I don't think making them *bigger* is such a good idea."

"True," I agreed. "We don't need the Burger brothers any bigger than they already are."

I shut my eyes and tried to think of terrible things Gene could do to the Burgers. But each time, I thought of ways Gene could get it wrong.

Jesse turned to me and smiled. "I've got it! We'll wish for Mike and Roy to be *terrified* of us—just the way we are!"

"Hmm . . . sounds good," I said.

"Every time they look at us, they'll shake from fear," Jesse continued excitedly. "Imagine them running away from us—the two shrimpiest kids in class!"

I thought it over. As hard as I tried, I couldn't think of any way Gene could mess it up. "It's perfect," I declared. "There's no way we could get hurt if we make that wish."

"All right!" Jesse pumped his fist in the air. "Let's make the wish right now! I can't wait!"

Jesse and I dragged Gene away from the TV pieces and brought him into my room.

"Okay, Gene, listen up. We have a very important wish to make," I shouted.

Gene held his ears. "Hoo. You don't have to yell. I'm not deaf, you know. Go ahead. Make your wish. But don't give me a headache first!"

"Sorry," I muttered. "I'm just a little excited."

"So—make a wish!" the genie demanded impatiently.

Jesse cleared his throat. "We wish for Mike and Roy Burger to be terrified of us."

"But you can't *change* us at all," I added. "They have to be scared of us *the way we are.*"

Gene bowed. "That's an easy one. A lot easier than putting the TV back together."

I bit my lip and waited for Gene to do his stuff— hoping he wouldn't mess up this time. I could feel my hands sweating. I wiped them on my jeans and crossed my fingers.

"Please, please let this work!" I begged.

Gene closed his eyes. He waved his arms and hips around in his crazy hula. In a moment, he turned himself into a cloud of sour purple smoke.

Jesse and I watched as the cloud drifted up to the ceiling and then floated out the window.

Jesse and I stood alone in the room. Gene had vanished.

"Jesse?" I asked quietly. "Is there anything wrong with me? Am I really huge or something?"

Jesse studied me. "Nope," he said. "How about me?"

"Same as ever," I replied.

We smiled at each other and then started to laugh.

"Nothing went wrong!" Jesse cried. "I bet it worked!"

I slapped Jesse a high-five. "By tomorrow, the Burger brothers will be totally afraid of us! I can't wait to go to school in the morning!"

13

The next day Jesse and I were so excited, we ran all the way to school.

"I can't wait to see them whimper and cry when we walk by!" Jesse exclaimed as we ran up the steps of Shadyside Middle School.

We hurried straight to our lockers. The Burger brothers usually wait for us there. They like to tease us first thing in the morning.

One morning last fall, they stuffed Jesse into his gym locker. They locked him in—and left him there to suffocate on the aroma of sweaty gym socks.

Another time they pushed me into the cutest boy in school, Dave Reynolds, and told him I was in love with him. I thought I was going to die!

But this morning they were nowhere in sight.

We waited at our lockers until right before the first bell.

As we headed to our classrooms, Jesse sighed. "The one morning I'm looking forward to seeing them—and they're late for school."

"Weird," I murmured.

Jesse chuckled. "Maybe they were too scared to get out of bed this morning."

I laughed too, thinking of the Burger brothers cringing and quaking under their sheets.

"Well, we'll definitely see them at lunch," I told Jesse. "Those big apes never miss a meal."

At lunchtime I sat with my friends Kristen and Laura at our usual table by the windows. While they talked about our math test, I scanned the lunchroom.

Sometimes Mike and Roy sat with the twins, Cornelia and Gabrielle Phillips. But today the twins were sitting by themselves, staring at one of those cool 3-D posters you have to cross your eyes to see.

Where are Mike and Roy? I wondered. Those two *never* skip school. They hate missing the chance to tease Jesse and me all day.

I caught sight of Jesse on my way out of the lunchroom.

"Where do you think they are?" I asked, jogging over to him.

"Maybe they're sick or something," Jesse offered.

As we walked out of the lunchroom, we spotted Roy and Mike's teacher leaving the teachers' lounge.

"Let's ask Ms. Hartman," Jesse suggested. "She probably knows where they are."

"Ms. Hartman, have you seen Mike and Roy today?" I called, trying not to sound too nervous.

"Funny you should ask," Ms. Hartman answered. "I was just wondering where those two might be. They didn't show up this morning. And their mother hasn't called to say they're sick. It's not like them."

A queasy feeling gripped my stomach. Something is wrong here, I thought. Very wrong.

"Well, if I hear anything about them, I'll let you know," I told Ms. Hartman.

"Why, thank you, Hannah. It's very nice of you to be so concerned about them." Ms. Hartman patted my shoulder.

Jesse and I said good-bye and hurried down the hall. "Gene messed up again," I whispered. "I know it."

"Maybe," Jesse said. "Or maybe Mike and Roy are just absent. It's kind of nice being able to walk the halls and not worry about running into them."

"True," I agreed. "But they're never absent. Never! Do you think that Gene—"

I didn't get to finish my question. The bell rang. We both hurried to our classrooms.

I kept thinking about the Burger brothers all afternoon.

Gene was supposed to make them terrified of Jesse and me. Were Mike and Roy too terrified to come to school?

Finally the bell rang at the end of the day.

I caught up to Jesse and his friends out front. As we began to walk home together, I told Jesse how I couldn't stop thinking about Mike and Roy.

"Don't worry about them." Jesse shrugged. "Do you think the Burger brothers would be worried about *us* if we were absent?"

"Probably not," I mumbled.

When we stepped to the edge of the school parking lot, Jesse stopped short. He pointed to a white station wagon. "Hey, that's Mom. What's she doing here?"

Mom rolled down the window and started waving frantically.

"What's going on?" I asked her as we piled in. "You never pick us up."

"Well, I was a little worried," Mom said, biting her bottom lip.

"Worried?" I demanded.

"I thought you two might be upset. You know. About those two boys in your school. The Burger brothers."

I gasped.

"What about them?" Jesse choked out. "What happened to them, Mom?"

14

"Didn't you hear?" Mom asked. "Didn't they tell you in school? The Burger brothers—they disappeared last night!"

I stared at the back of Mom's head as we drove along in silence.

Disappeared.

The word bounced around in my brain over and over again.

Disappeared, disappeared, disappeared.

Jesse sat in the front seat with Mom. He didn't say a word the whole ride home.

Mom peered at me through the rearview mirror. "I'm sorry if I scared you two. Everyone *is* very concerned. Promise me you'll be careful."

"We promise," I murmured.

"Yeah," Jesse echoed. "We promise."

We'd *better* be careful, I thought. Because of us, there's a crazy genie on the loose.

A genie who made two boys disappear!

Jesse and I went straight from the car to my studio in the garage. Once Mom was in the house, I slumped down in an old armchair in the corner.

"It's all our fault!" I wailed. "We made a wish— and Gene made them disappear!"

"But that isn't what we wished!" Jesse cried. "It's not really our fault!"

"Of course it is!" I moaned. I stood up and paced the floor, thinking.

"We have to get Gene back here," I decided finally. "He has to tell us what he did."

Jesse unfolded a beach chair and plopped down on it. "Why?" he asked. "The Burger brothers are finally out of our lives for good. I think it's great!"

"But, Jesse," I argued, "what about *Mrs.* Burger? She's always so nice to us. I'll bet she's freaking out right now."

"I suppose." Jesse sighed. "All right. Let's get Gene back here. He still owes us a wish anyway."

"No more wishes!" I begged. "Gene doesn't know what he's doing. He's too dangerous."

"So we won't wish for anything dangerous,"

Jesse argued. "We'll wish for new bikes or something. That can't hurt us."

"Gene will find *some* way to mess it up!" I cried. "He'll make the bikes bigger than our house! Or they'll have a mind of their own and take us where we don't want to go! We are not making *any* wishes. All we're going to do now is call for Gene. And make him bring back Mike and Roy—wherever they are."

Jesse frowned. "Well, how do we call him? It's not like he has a phone."

"Hmmmm." I thought about it for a few moments. Then I had an idea.

I ran inside the house. Seconds later, I came back carrying the little portable TV Mom keeps in the kitchen. I set the TV on a box and plugged it in. I turned it on and cranked up the volume.

"Gene! Geeeeene!" I called. "Would you like to see how *this* TV works?"

We waited. Soon a wisp of purple smoke drifted into the garage from outside. A few seconds later Gene stood before us.

"You're here!" Jesse cried.

"Can I really take apart this TV?" Gene asked eagerly. "It's so small. I'm pretty sure I could put *this* one back together."

"Not so fast," I said, stepping between Gene and

the TV. "What did you do to the Burger brothers? They disappeared last night."

"They did?" Gene's eyes bulged in surprise. "Hoo! They disappeared? But I wanted to make them small and weak—so they would be terrified of you."

"You made them *disappear*," I accused Gene sternly.

"Wow." The genie shook his purple head. "I am *sooo* out of practice." He sighed. "All those years in the bottle. You get a little rusty—you know? Oh, well . . . those are the breaks—huh?"

I struggled to keep calm. "Gene, please, you've got to do something about Mike and Roy. You have to find them."

Gene narrowed his eyes at me. "You're not happy? You want them back?"

"Yes," I replied. "It isn't right. You can't just make two kids disappear."

"Whatever," he muttered. He stood straight and closed his eyes. He reached his arms out to the open garage door and chanted something in another language.

Gene swayed his arms and hips from side to side as he chanted.

Nothing happened.

No Burgers anywhere.

69

Were they *really* gone forever?

Then I caught a flash of movement at the doorway.

Two baby bunnies hopped up the driveway. They stared at Jesse and me.

As I walked closer, their furry little bodies trembled with fear.

"Yo!" one of them whispered.

"Hey—yo!" the other bunny mouthed.

I gasped. No way.

It couldn't be!

"Jesse! I—I think it's Mike and Roy!" I stammered.

"Excuse me?" Jesse stepped up beside me, his eyes on the bunnies.

"Yo!" one of the bunnies whispered.

"Yo—hey!" the other coughed.

"Oh, wow—it's true!" Jesse cried. "It *is* Mike and Roy!"

Gene laughed. "See? My magic *did* work! I made them into timid little bunny rabbits! Now, every time they see you, they will be afraid of you! Hoo! I wish I could kiss myself! I am good. I am *good!*"

Jesse dropped to his knees. He stared down at the trembling bunnies. *"Boooo!"* he screamed.

The bunnies froze in terror.

Jesse laughed. "Ha! See how that feels, you creeps?"

"Gene, you've got to turn them back!" I cried. "They can't stay like that!"

Gene's mouth dropped open in surprise. "Huh? I did what you wished."

"No. It's no good!" I cried. "Turn them back. Turn them back—now!"

"Nope," Gene replied coolly. "No way."

15

"**E**xcuse me?" I cried.

Gene shrugged. "Rules are rules. I cannot turn the bunnies back into boys unless you wish for it. You've got to use your third wish."

"Hey—no way!" Jesse cried.

"It isn't fair!" I agreed. "We never asked for this," I said, pointing to the two frightened bunnies.

"Ah, but you did." Gene wagged his finger at me. "You said you wanted these guys to be frightened of you just the way you are of them. And now they are! You should be congratulating me. Hoo. I'm good!"

I turned to Jesse. "We don't have a choice. We have to use our third wish."

"Whoa." Jesse groaned. "What do you mean? Use our *last wish* for the Burger brothers? Uhh-uhh!" He shook his head.

"Would you *really* leave them the way they are?" I asked.

Jesse reached down and stroked one of the bunny's ears. "They're definitely cuter this way," he argued. "And besides, think about all the kids at school who won't be bullied anymore."

"Jesse, we can't do this. Not even to Mike and Roy," I scolded.

Jesse sighed. "Yeah, I guess so. Go ahead and turn them back to their nasty old selves. See if I care."

I turned to Gene. "Okay, turn them back. And do it right this time. Don't change me into Mike or Roy or something."

"Whatever you say, master. This is your last wish." Gene stood up and stretched. He closed his eyes and went into his trance, waving his arms and doing his crazy hula dance.

When we saw the purple smoke swirling toward us from outside, Jesse and I braced ourselves. As it came closer, it whipped up papers and paintbrushes in the garage. Rakes and ladders fell off their hooks and flew through the air.

I ran into the corner. Jesse followed. We crouched there together, ducking for cover.

I couldn't see the bunnies through the purple smoke. Finally the smoke swirled out of the garage. I let out a sigh of relief as it lifted up into the sky.

The Burger brothers stood in the doorway of the garage, hugging each other. Their eyes were bulging, and their faces were chalk white.

"L-let's get out of here," Roy squeaked. He grabbed Mike's hand. The two boys ran out of our garage—like two scared rabbits.

I frowned as I watched them run down the street. "They could have *thanked* us," I muttered. "But I guess they were too scared."

"Well," Gene said, rubbing his hands together, "I'm sorry to say, that was your last wish."

"Boy, were we cheated," Jesse griped. He slumped back into the beach chair.

"That's okay. I'm glad," I said. I held up Gene's bottle. "Now—time to go back where you came from."

I couldn't wait to get that genie out of our lives forever.

Gene waved his hands as if shooing away the bottle. "Put that thing down. I'm not going in there."

"Huh?" I gaped at him. "But—but—"

"I told you," the genie insisted, "I am never going back into that bottle again."

"What do you mean?" I asked. I pictured Gene

spending the rest of his life in our house, taking apart the TV sets and eating all the pizzas. There was no way I would let that happen!

"I explained it to you," the genie insisted. "I'm never going back in. We made a deal. One of *you* has to go into the bottle now."

16

"**O**nce you've used all your wishes, one of *you* must take my place in the bottle," Gene said calmly.

For a second I couldn't breathe. I felt as though someone had kicked me in the stomach.

"Wh-what are you talking about?" I finally choked out.

The genie narrowed his purple eyes at me. "One of *you* must take my place in the bottle," he repeated. "You must choose which of you it will be."

"But—why?" My legs felt all wobbly. I flopped down into the old armchair.

"That is your payment for the three wishes. One

of you will live in the bottle . . . until the end of time!" The genie rose up over Jesse and me. "A deal is a deal."

"But you never told us that!" I shrieked. "You never explained that!"

He rubbed his chin. "Didn't I? Oh . . . guess I forgot. Sorry about that."

"But—but—but—" I sputtered, feeling total panic sweep over me.

"I explained now," Gene said, frowning. "Better late than never, huh?"

He grabbed the bottle from my hand and held it up. "Who is it going to be? Hannah or Jesse?"

I swallowed hard. My throat felt as if it had been tied in a knot.

I turned to Jesse. The color completely drained out of his face. "We never would have agreed to that!" Jesse cried.

"How could you do this to us?" I demanded. "We thought you were our friend!"

"I'm a genie. Not a friend," Gene replied with a shrug. "It's a job, you know."

"But we can't!" Jesse protested.

"It's not so bad," Gene told him. "It's a perfectly nice bottle. A little cramped, maybe. But it's warm and dry in there. After a while you forget your old life completely."

I rubbed my hands over my face. My skin felt cold and clammy.

"Maybe you'll get lucky," Gene continued. "Maybe your bottle will smash against some rocks someday. Set you free. It could happen."

We're doomed, I thought glumly.

"You can't do this to us!" Jesse shouted. "We've been your friends! We let you stay in our house! And now—"

Gene clapped his hands sharply. "Quiet! I'm getting a headache from all this talk."

"But, please—" I started to say.

"You are no longer my masters," the genie said sternly. "I do not have to listen to you any longer."

Gene floated up from the floor. And as he floated, he grew. Purple waves of energy sparked off him. His face turned dark and menacing.

"You must choose now!" he roared. "Which one of you goes into the bottle? *Which one?*"

17

"**W**e—we need time to decide," I said.

I was stalling for time. Jesse and I had to go somewhere and think. Think of a way *out* of this mess.

"Fine. I can give you until midnight," the genie replied.

He rose up over Jesse and me. I stared into his watery purple eyes. All I saw there was evil. Pure evil. Why hadn't I seen it before?

"Till midnight," the genie offered. "That's fair enough."

"What if we refuse to go along with this?" Jesse demanded in a trembling voice. "What if we don't decide who goes in the bottle?"

Anger crossed the genie's face. "Then *I* shall make the decision for you!" he bellowed. "There is no way out of this. One of you must go in the bottle."

He waved his arms in the air. His body slowly faded into a thick purple cloud of smoke.

"Wait! Where are you going?" I cried.

"Don't worry," he whispered as the cloud floated out the door. "I'll be back at midnight!"

Jesse and I headed up to my room. I brought the bottle and set it on my dresser.

I sprawled tensely on my bed with my hands behind my head. Barky curled up next to me.

"It's all your fault!" Jesse cried. He straddled my desk chair and stared at me angrily.

"My fault? How is it *my* fault?" I demanded.

"You just had to pick up that bottle, didn't you? If you didn't fish that bottle out of the lake, we wouldn't be in this mess."

"Do I need to remind you who *opened* the stupid bottle?" I shot back. I sighed. "It doesn't matter whose fault it is. What matters is finding a way out of this. What are we going to do?"

"We have no choice," Jesse replied solemnly. "We need help. We have to tell Mom and Dad the whole story."

* * *

The two of us sat at the dinner table in silence.

"You two are awfully quiet," Mom said. "Anything wrong?"

I glanced across the table at Jesse. He was shoveling a big forkful of spaghetti into his mouth. I guessed I was going to have to tell them.

I cleared my throat. "Well, actually, there *is* something wrong," I began to explain.

Mom and Dad stopped eating to look at me.

"Remember that kid Gene?" I asked.

They nodded.

"Well, he's not really a kid," I continued. I took a deep breath. I wanted to get it out all at once. "He's really a genie. A genie who lives in a bottle. I found the bottle in Fear Lake. Jesse and I opened it and Gene popped out. He gave us three wishes, and now he wants one of us to go live in the bottle!"

I stopped—and stared at my parents. Waiting for them to react.

Dad laughed first. Then Mom joined in.

"That Gene was a pretty weird kid," Dad declared. "But he's a little too big to fit in a bottle!"

That made Mom and Dad laugh even harder.

They don't believe me, I realized. *Of course* they don't believe me! Who would believe such a crazy story?

"Um, Jesse?" I whispered. I hoped he would back me up. Tell them I wasn't joking.

But to my shock, Jesse's eyes were wide with fear. His mouth hung open.

I turned to the dining room window to see what he was staring at.

The purple genie, hovering in the evening air, glaring through the window at us angrily.

I started to choke from fright. I grabbed my water, took a long gulp, and pointed to the window.

Barky growled from under the table.

"Hannah—what's wrong?" Dad asked.

"Dad—look!" I frantically pointed to the window. "There he is! There!"

But the genie had vanished.

"I—I don't see anyone," Dad said, staring hard.

"Why are you two so full of jokes tonight?" Mom demanded. "It isn't April Fools'—is it?"

"No," I replied softly. I stared down at my uneaten spaghetti. It was no use. I would never get my parents to believe us.

Jesse and I helped with the dishes. Then we trudged back up to my room.

"That was a complete waste of time." Jesse sighed. He plopped down on the edge of my bed. "We need a Plan B."

I glanced over at my night table. My eyes went wide. "Hey—I think I've got one!" I told my brother.

18

Jesse sat straight up. "You do? What is it?"

I crossed the room to the night table. I picked up Gene's bottle. "If Gene can't find the bottle, he can't put us in it—right?"

"You're *right!*" Jesse cried. "He left the bottle with us! How stupid of him! Let's get rid of it—right now!"

I tensely twirled a strand of hair around my finger. Where was the best place to hide the bottle?

My bedroom was pretty messy, but it was way too small. Gene could search it in a second.

"Ark! Ark! Ark!" Barky yapped, trotting into my room.

I smiled. I thought of a place Gene would never find his bottle.

"What if we buried it?" I asked my brother. "We'll dig a hole in the backyard and bury it there."

"Perfect!" Jesse agreed.

We grabbed the bottle and raced out to the garage, where we found two old shovels.

I handed a shovel to Jesse. "Better dig behind the garage so Mom and Dad won't see," I instructed.

We crept behind the garage and chose a spot. I pushed my shovel into the dirt. We worked as quickly as we could, digging a hole behind some bushes.

By the time we finished, the hole was at least two feet deep.

Jesse wiped his damp face on his sleeve. "Okay, dump the bottle in there."

I tossed the bottle into the hole. We stared down at it for a second. Then we covered it with dirt.

I wiped my dirty hands on my jeans. "Done!" I cried, slapping Jesse a high-five.

Then we carried the shovels back into the garage.

What a relief! I thought. I trudged up the stairs to my room. "I can't wait until Gene shows up at midnight!" I declared. "I can't wait to see the look on his face when he sees that the bottle is gone!"

"Me too!" Jesse replied, grinning.

I opened the door to my room.

And gasped in horror.

"No!" I moaned. "This can't be happening! It *can't* be!"

19

"How did *that* get here?" Jesse cried.

"I—I don't know," I replied in a quivering voice.

We both stared at the brown bottle. It stood on my night table. Right where it had stood before.

"Oh, Jesse." I sighed. "What are we going to do now?"

He shook his head. "Maybe we can find a better hiding place. You know. Someplace a lot farther away."

I swallowed hard. My mouth felt as dry as cotton. "But what if that doesn't work? We don't have much time left!"

Jesse opened his mouth to answer. But he stopped—and gaped at the open bedroom window.

I turned to see wisps of purple smoke drift in from outside.

Oh, no! I thought. Please—not yet! We're not ready!

The purple smoke filled the room. Then the genie began to take shape.

"Why are you here?" I demanded. "It's not midnight yet! We still have time!"

The genie rose up over us. He held a gold pocket watch in his gnarled hand. He held it up to his ear.

"Hoo. Guess my watch is fast," he said, shaking it. "I've got twelve midnight—on the nose." He held it up to show us.

"Well, you have to go away!" I cried. "You said you would give us more time!"

The genie slid the watch into his loose purple robe. He narrowed his eyes at us. "I changed my mind. You've had enough time."

He floated over us. "Which will it be? Hannah or Jesse?"

I uttered a gasp of horror.

He's going to put one of us in that bottle right now! I realized.

I have to do something!

My eyes darted around the room. The bottle! I'll break it into a million pieces.

I took a deep breath. And dove to the night table.

My fingers curled around the bottle. I drew my arm back—and heaved it at the wall.

"Nooooooo!" the genie shrieked.

20

~~~

The bottle shattered. Shards of glass flew everywhere.

"What have you done?" the genie shrieked.

My heart beat wildly. *I did it! I really did it!*

"Go, Hannah!" Jesse cried.

Gene shook his head sadly. "Don't you realize what a waste of time that was?"

I gaped at him. "Excuse me?"

He waved his hands and did a short dance.

"Oh, nooo!" Jesse and I groaned.

Jagged pieces of brown glass flew up from the floor. As the genie danced and waved his hands, the glass rose up to the night table.

And formed a perfect bottle again.

The genie stopped his dance. His smile faded. His eyes glowed with anger. And evil.

"Don't try anything else," he warned. "I'm losing patience with you. A deal is a deal—remember?"

"Right," I agreed. I glanced at my clock. "A deal is a deal. And it's only ten till midnight. Jesse and I have ten more minutes. You gave us till midnight. A deal is a deal."

The genie tossed up his hands. "Okay, okay. I can take a hint. I'll go. But I'll be back. Don't try to escape. And don't try to bury the bottle again. Hoo. I'll have to get tough with you. No more Mr. Nice Guy."

In a swirl of purple smoke, he floated back out the window.

I ran to the window, slammed it, and locked it.

"Now what?" Jesse cried in a tiny voice.

I had only one thought. We had to run. We had to get out of there—as far away from the genie as we could.

I sprinted over to my closet, tugged out a sweat-shirt, and pulled it on. "We have no choice. We have to run," I told Jesse.

"But—but—" Jesse started to protest.

"Can you think of anything else?" I demanded.

He shook his head. He knew I was right. It was the only thing left for us to do.

"Go get a sweatshirt," I ordered. "We don't have much time."

"But where can we go?" Jesse cried.

Think, Hannah. Think hard. Where *can* you go?

"We'll head for the woods," I decided. "There are lots of good places to hide there."

"The Fear Street woods?" Jesse whispered with a shudder.

I nodded solemnly. "The Fear Street woods."

Barky wagged his tail furiously when he saw us sneaking down the stairs.

"Oh, no," Jesse moaned. "He'll bark like crazy when we leave. He'll wake Mom and Dad."

"I already thought of that," I replied in a whisper. I went into the kitchen and took three doggie treats out of the box.

"Here you go, Barky," I called, setting the treats down on the floor.

As Barky gobbled up the treats, I motioned for Jesse to follow me out of the house. Barky didn't even raise his head when we left.

Neither of us said a word as we jogged toward the woods.

We got there quickly. Moonlight washed over the black, gnarled trees, casting eerie shadows. Animals cried and howled all around us. Strange howls that sent cold shivers down my back.

"I don't know, Hannah, maybe this isn't such a good idea," Jesse whispered.

I glanced at my watch. Nearly midnight. "We don't have any other choice," I told Jesse, pushing a branch out of my way.

I gasped when something brushed up against my leg.

"What was that?" I leapt back.

Two green eyes glowed up at me in the darkness.

A cat. Only a cat.

"Go away, kitty." I nudged it away with my foot. It scampered off into the trees.

"Hannah, do you hear something?" Jesse asked.

I stopped and listened. The wind whispered through the trees behind us. An animal howled somewhere nearby.

"Hey, let's go back," Jesse pleaded. "I don't like this, Hannah. This is a bad plan."

"Yes, it is a *terrible* plan," a voice rasped.

I whirled around.

The genie floated right behind us!

"It is midnight," he said softly.

21

The genie reached a gnarled hand toward me.

"No!" I wailed.

I could feel the shock of purple waves that vibrated around him. The woods glowed eerily. We were all bathed in purple light.

"We won't go—" Jesse cried, stepping up close to me.

The genie shook his head. His eyes glowed like giant fireflies. "Hoo. I was afraid of this. I'll have to make the choice myself."

He grabbed me by the shoulders. "Hannah— into the bottle."

"No!" I shrieked. With a desperate jerk, I tugged free.

"Jesse—run!" I screamed.

We both turned—and ran.

But a swirl of purple followed us. The genie floated in front of us.

"This way!" I cried, spinning my brother around.

We turned and ran toward a clump of low willows.

The genie floated easily in front of us.

He shook his head almost sadly. "Trying to run from a genie? Can you think of a bigger waste of time?"

Jesse and I ignored him. We leapt over a fallen log and dove behind a thick clump of evergreen bushes.

But the genie was ahead of us, hovering over the ground. Waiting for us.

"I can turn you to stone," he threatened, eyes glowing brightly, lips curled in a sneer. "It's one of my better tricks."

Jesse and I huddled together, gasping for breath.

Stone, I thought.

Stone.

Yes. Stone.

The genie had given me an idea.

But how could Jesse and I escape in order to try it?

"Hannah—" he rasped. "Hannah—it's time."

The genie raised the brown bottle up to me.

"Say good-bye to your brother," he whispered. "And make it quick. Your new home is waiting for you."

22

I stared at the bottle hovering in front of my face.

I tried to picture myself folded up inside it. Floating. Bobbing in the water. Forever and ever.

"But I get seasick!" I blurted out.

The genie didn't reply. He shoved the bottle closer.

How can we escape? I asked myself. How can we get to the garage so that I can try my plan?

No way, I realized.

Jesse and I were trapped. Defeated.

It was over. . . .

"Hey—yo!" A voice interrupted my terrifying thoughts.

"Yo!"

I turned to see the Burger brothers leap out from behind the evergreen bushes.

"Hoo!" the genie cried, as startled as Jesse and I. "It's the bunny boys!"

Mike and Roy stopped in shock as they saw the genie.

"What are you two doing out in the woods?" I cried.

"Looking for people to scare," Mike replied.

"We howl like animals and frighten people," Roy explained.

Mike raised a big net. "And I like to capture insects and torture them," he said. "It's kind of a hobby."

"I liked you better as bunnies," the genie chimed in.

"Yo! Get him!" Roy cried suddenly.

Mike moved quickly. He raised the big insect net—and swooped it down over the startled genie's head.

The genie was so surprised—and Mike was so strong—that he pushed the genie to the ground.

This was our chance. "Jesse—run!" I screamed.

We both took off toward home.

I called out thanks to the Burger brothers.

"Thanks for changing us back to humans!" Roy called.

Well . . . they're *almost* human, I thought.

And I'd never been so glad to see them.

But how long could they hold the genie under the net?

Could Jesse and I get to the garage in time?

23

As we ran desperately through the woods, I tried to explain my plan to Jesse.

"We'll keep the garage dark," I said breathlessly. "I'll stand my sculpture of you behind the worktable. I'll tell the genie that you are the one we picked to go in the bottle."

"Huh? Me?" Jesse gasped, leaping over a tall, round rock. "Why does it have to be *me?*"

"It won't really be you," I told him, panting hard as I ran. The back of the garage came into view. "You hide in the back of the garage. We want the genie to think that the sculpture is you. We want the genie to put the *sculpture* in the bottle. That way, we'll be safe."

We reached the front of the garage, gasping and panting.

"Will it work?" Jesse asked. "Will it fool him?"

"I don't know," I replied, struggling to catch my breath. "Maybe if it's dark enough, he'll fall for it."

I swallowed hard. "Maybe . . ." I crossed my fingers and prayed for good luck.

We both hoisted up the garage door.

I moved quickly to my worktable. I uncovered my life-size sculpture of Jesse.

The nose still wasn't right. But it was too late to worry about that.

Jesse hid behind the cartons in the back of the garage.

I heard a whisper of wind. Then saw the swirling purple smoke.

The genie floated quickly into the garage, his robe flowing around him. His eyes flashed purple, like two coals in a dying fire.

"Those bunny boys are strong," he rasped. "But not strong enough to hold a wisp of smoke."

"What did you do to them?" I demanded. "Did you turn them back into bunnies?"

He frowned. "That would be a waste of magic. I just left them there in the woods, swinging their net, wondering how I got away. Hoo. They looked very confused."

His expression changed. "I needed to save my

magic. It takes a lot of strength to squeeze you into the bottle."

He floated closer. I could feel the electric purple waves shooting off his body.

"Are you ready, Hannah?" he demanded, reaching out a hand. "Are you through trying to escape? Are you ready to enter your new home?"

"Uh . . . well . . . there's been a change of plan," I told him.

He raised one purple eyebrow. "A change of plan?"

I nodded. I gestured to the Jesse sculpture, standing so still behind the worktable. "Jesse is going into the bottle," I announced in a choked whisper. "He—he's being very brave."

I pretended to cry. "Jesse has decided he will be the one," I told the genie. I let out a sob. I made my shoulders tremble.

The genie turned to the figure of Jesse. He narrowed his eyes at it, squinting into the deep darkness.

Would he fall for my trick?

Would he believe that was Jesse standing there?

24

I backed up to the full-length mirror. I stopped when I felt the mirror press against my back.

My eyes moved from the genie to the Jesse sculpture.

In the darkness of the garage, the sculpture looked so real, so lifelike.

But it stood so still. As still as a statue.

How bad was the old genie's eyesight?

Would he believe it was Jesse?

Would he put the sculpture in the bottle? Then go away and never come back?

I sucked in my breath as the genie floated closer to the worktable. He stared hard at the sculpture. Squinted at it for what seemed like hours!

"It won't be so bad, Jesse," he told it. "It's a little cramped in there. And there's no bathroom. But after a hundred years or so . . . you'll get used to it."

It's working! I thought, crossing my fingers again. *It's working!*

The genie lowered the bottle to the garage floor in front of him.

Then he raised both hands. And began to chant.

"Good-bye, Jesse," I cried, sobbing loudly. "Good-bye. I'll miss you. I really will."

I pretended to cry loudly. I covered my face with both hands and let out sob after sob.

But all the while, I had my eyes on the genie.

As the genie chanted, he swayed from side to side.

His voice grew louder. Stronger.

Clouds of purple floated around and around the garage. The purple mist floated around the bottle on the floor. And around my sculpture.

The genie waved his hands and swayed harder.

He chanted even louder.

Then he suddenly stopped.

The purple clouds vanished.

I gaped at him in shock. "What's wrong?" I whispered.

He turned to me. Even in the darkness of the garage I could see the anger on his twisted features.

"My eyesight is pretty bad, Hannah," he rasped. "But not *that* bad."

"Wh-what do you mean?" I stammered hoarsely.

"That's not Jesse," the genie cried angrily. "That's your clay sculpture."

He raised both hands toward me. His eyes glowed so brightly, they lit up the garage.

"Your little trick didn't work, Hannah," the genie whispered. "Now you will have to pay."

25

"**N**ow you're going in the bottle! Have a pleasant journey, Hannah," the genie cried.

He raised his hands toward me and began to chant.

He swayed his whole body and chanted louder.

I could see the purple clouds rising all around.

My eyes lowered to the brown bottle. I saw wisps of purple float around it.

I suddenly felt drawn to it. I could feel myself being pulled . . . pulled to the bottle.

I raised my eyes and saw the purple mist shooting toward me. Shooting from the genie's outstretched hands.

Like purple lightning. Aimed at me.

Pulling me. Pulling me to the bottle . . .

The genie's chant became a scream. He waved both hands hard.

Shot a final purple bolt of electricity at me.

I took a deep breath—

And ducked.

I hit the garage floor and rolled away.

And turned in time to see the bolt of purple lightning hit the full-length mirror that was behind me.

The lightning bounced off the mirror—and shot back to the genie.

Surrounded him. Swirled over him.

The genie blazed in purple light. A light so bright, I had to shield my eyes.

"Nooooooo!" I heard his scream of horror.

I opened my eyes in time to see the genie shrink inside the purple electricity. Shrink . . . shrink . . . into the brown bottle.

With a desperate leap, I dove to the floor—and shoved the cork deep into the bottle opening.

The bottle shook hard in my hand.

And then lay still.

Jesse crawled out from behind the cartons. "Wow!" he murmured. "Wow! How did you do that, Hannah?"

105

I struggled to catch my breath as I climbed to my feet. "I ducked," I told Jesse. "That's all. I ducked—and the genie cast his spell on himself."

Jesse stared down at the brown bottle. So still. So silent.

So harmless now.

"Whew!" He sighed. "My legs are still trembling." He slapped me a high-five. "You did it! You did it!"

I picked up the bottle. "I won't feel safe until this is back in Fear Lake," I said with a shudder.

"You mean—" Jesse started to say.

I nodded. "Yes. We have to take it there—right now. I have to know that it's gone forever."

We were both weary and shaken. But we headed back through the Fear Street woods anyway.

I carried the bottle tightly in two hands. I wanted to run to the lake and toss the bottle away as fast as I could. But I walked slowly and carefully.

I didn't want to accidentally break the bottle and let the genie escape.

"Do you believe the Burger brothers actually helped us?" Jesse said as we made our way to the lakeshore.

"Yes. We kind of got our wish after all!" I

exclaimed. "I mean, they are our friends now. We don't have to be afraid of them anymore."

"Weird," Jesse replied, shaking his head. "I guess the genie came through for us in a way."

I didn't care. When we reached the edge of the lake, sparkling like silver under the pale moonlight, I pulled back my arm—and heaved the bottle as high and as far as I could.

It sailed out far. And hit the water with a solid *plunk*.

Water splashed up around it.

The bottle sunk below the surface. Then I saw it bob back up to the top.

Jesse and I both let out happy cheers. We actually hugged each other—something we haven't done since I was four!

We did a happy dance of celebration. Tossing each other around. Our shoes slapping the wet mud of the lakeshore.

I stopped dancing when I tripped over something.

I caught my balance and gazed down.

"What *is* that?" I cried.

Jesse bent and picked it up. It was a lamp. A strangely shaped brass lamp.

"Weird," Jesse murmured, holding it up close to his face with both hands.

"It's like those magic lamps in fairy tales," I told him. "You know. The kind you rub, and you get three wishes. And . . ."

"No, Jesse!" I cried. "No—*don't!* What are you doing? Don't rub it! DON'T! DON'T RUB IT!"

Too late.

Are you ready for another walk
down Fear Street?
Turn the page for a terrifying
sneak preview.

R·L·STINE'S
GHOSTS of FEAR STREET ® #20

SPELL OF THE
SCREAMING JOKERS

Coming mid-April 1997

When Max finished dealing, we picked up our hands.

"Have fun, kids!" Mrs. Davidson said, and she left the room.

I studied my cards one at a time. Two of clubs. Six of hearts. Three of diamonds. Jack of clubs.

A horrible scream split the air!

I jumped.

Frankie dropped his cards to the floor.

"Frankie!" I exclaimed, startled. "What's wrong?"

Frankie's eyes stared, wide open.

His jaw dropped.

And he let out the most horrifying scream I'd ever heard.

"Frankie!" I cried out again. "What's wrong! Tell us—what's wrong!"

Frankie turned to me—and the screaming stopped. Stopped suddenly, as if a knife sliced it off mid-scream.

Mrs. Davidson ran into Max's room. "What happened?" she cried. "Is someone hurt?"

We shook our heads.

"Who screamed?" she asked.

"Frankie did," Louisa told her.

"No, I didn't," Frankie said.

"Yes, you did!" Louisa exclaimed. "Your mouth was wide open. We all heard you. Screaming like a maniac."

"I wasn't screaming," Frankie said flatly.

"Yeah, right," I said. "You nearly burst my eardrums. You dropped your cards—then you started screaming."

"I . . . wasn't . . . screaming," Frankie said slowly. "I dropped my cards because of—because of the joker."

Frankie glanced under the table. I followed his gaze.

There his cards lay—all facedown. All but one. All but the joker.

The joker—it was like no joker we had ever seen.

It had huge round eyes that bulged right out of their sockets. Hideous eyes! I felt as if they could *see* me!

Its bright red lips curved up in a crooked, evil smile.

It wore a floppy green cap with three silver bells on the top.

In its hand, the joker held a stick. On the top of the stick sat a skull. A skull with eyes that glowed like hot coals!

I started to turn away—when the joker's face began to move!

Its eyeballs darted left and right! First it peered at me. Then it glared at Louisa. Then Jeff.

The joker's eyeballs came to rest on Frankie. Its mouth twisted open—in a grin full of yellow, jagged teeth.

The joker flapped its big ears. It rattled its stick—and the skull's eyes flashed sparks!

I stared in horror. I couldn't speak.

"What's wrong?" Max's mom asked. "What are you looking at?"

At the sound of her voice, the joker's ugly face froze.

Had it really moved?

Or had I imagined it?

I glanced at my friends. Had they seen it move?

I couldn't tell. They were all staring at the door. At Max's mom as she entered the room.

Mrs. Davidson picked up the card. "What a horrible card!" she cried. She gathered up the other cards from the floor.

"Let me have all the cards, kids," she said. "I'll check to make sure there aren't any more jokers. How in the world did this terrible-looking thing get into the deck in the first place?"

Max only shrugged as he handed his mom his cards. He didn't seem very upset about the joker. Maybe his doctor told him not to get too excited— about anything.

But I was plenty excited. My heart was racing!

Frankie's eyes met mine. His wide-open eyes— filled with fright now.

I turned to Jeff. It was hard to tell if he was scared or not. He still had on his sunglasses.

"That was horrible," I said. I didn't know whether I had seen the joker move or not. "That wasn't a regular joker. No wonder you screamed."

"I told you—I didn't scream," Frankie said.

"Come on, Frankie," I said. "Just admit it. We all heard you. I bet the whole neighborhood heard you."

"I didn't scream." Frankie glared at me. "So quit saying I did."

"There. I've checked the deck. There aren't any more ugly jokers," Mrs. Davidson interrupted our argument.

She handed the deck of cards to Max. "Remember, it's good card manners to let someone cut the cards, Max."

Max began shuffling.

"Um . . . you really still want to play?" I asked.

Max shrugged. "Why not?"

"Yes, but . . ." I began. I stopped. With the jokers out of the deck, I guess it was okay to play.

We played hand after hand of Hearts. By the time the four of us left Max's house, I saw clubs and diamonds, hearts and spades swimming before my eyes.

And I still saw that ugly joker. Saw its evil grin. Saw it move.

How could a single card be so frightening?

How?

"I wish we'd left earlier," Louisa grumbled as we walked along Fear Street in the dark. "I hate this street at night."

"It seems like the streetlights are always broken here," I complained. "I can't see a thing!"

"We could always cut through Mrs. Murder's yard again," Frankie suggested.

"Fat chance," I said. Then I heard something. "Hey, listen. What's that?"

I glanced in the direction of Mrs. Marder's house. But it was too dark to see anything.

"I hear something rattling," Jeff whispered.

Rattling—that was the sound I heard. Rattling—like someone shaking a can full of pebbles.

"I hear it," Louisa added. "Listen. It's getting louder."

My eyes searched the shadows along Fear Street.

"Hey!" Frankie yelled suddenly. "Watch it, buddy!"

I whirled around.

I saw Frankie sprawled on the sidewalk.

A small figure bent over him. Probably the kid who knocked him down. Now he was saying something to Frankie.

"Frankie!" Louisa called. "Are you okay?"

Frankie didn't answer.

The figure straightened up. He wasn't very tall. He wore a green hat with a brim pulled down low over his forehead. I couldn't make out his face under the brim. The only thing I could see clearly was the stick he held in his hand.

I ran toward Frankie—and the shadowy figure rattled his stick fiercely. He let out a scream—and raced away into the darkness.

"Frankie, are you okay?" I asked. "Who was that?"

"I don't know, some little kid," Frankie groaned. "Boy, for a little kid he sure slammed into me hard!" Frankie rubbed his arm.

The four of us walked close together as we made our way along Fear Street.

"He said something weird," Frankie began as we headed home. "It sounded like, 'We shake the skull . . .' No. That wasn't it."

Frankie frowned, trying to remember. "I know. 'We shake the skull with eyes that gleam.'"

"That doesn't make any sense," Jeff said.

Frankie shrugged. "That's what it sounded like."

"That can't be what he said. Maybe he said something like, 'sorry to shake you up,'" Louisa suggested.

"No. That's not what he said." Frankie sounded definite.

That didn't stop Louisa. "Maybe the skull part was about how he hoped you didn't crack *your* skull."

Frankie groaned. "Louisa. Do me a favor. Stop guessing."

We didn't talk the rest of the way to Frankie's house. I had to admit, Louisa's explanations were pretty lame.

"Thanks," he said before going inside. "And—I'm sorry about getting you guys in trouble."

By the porch light, I saw that Frankie was pretty scraped up.

The side of his face was raw where he'd hit the pavement. And there was a strange, dark bruise above his wrist. It looked almost as if it were in the shape of a flower . . . or something.

"Frankie, that bruise . . ." I pointed to his arm. "It's shaped like . . . a club," I said, suddenly seeing it.

"A club?" Frankie studied the bruise. "What do you mean?"

"You know—the card suit," I said. "Like clubs, spades, hearts."

"Huh?" He grabbed the side of his arm and stared at the bruise.

Why does Frankie suddenly have a club on his arm? I wondered.

Something strange is going on here, I told myself. Something *very* strange.

About R. L. Stine

R. L. Stine, the creator of *Ghosts of Fear Street,* has written almost 100 scary novels for kids. The *Ghosts of Fear Street* series, like the *Fear Street* series, takes place in Shadyside and centers on the scary events that happen to people on Fear Street.

When he isn't writing, R. L. Stine likes to play pinball on his very own pinball machine, and explore New York City with his wife, Jane, and fifteen-year-old son, Matt.

WIN A TRIP TO MEET
R·L·STINE
...IF YOU DARE!
You could win an exciting weekend in New York City and have lunch with R.L. Stine

1 GRAND PRIZE: A WEEKEND (3 DAY/2 NIGHT) TRIP TO NEW YORK CITY TO MEET R.L. STINE
10 First Prizes: Walkman and an autographed "Ghosts of Fear Street" Audiobook
20 Second Prizes: Autographed "Ghosts of Fear Street" T-Shirt
30 Third Prizes: Autographed "Ghosts of Fear Street" Audiobook
50 Fourth Prizes: Autographed "Ghosts of Fear Street" Book
100 Fifth Prizes: "Ghosts of Fear Street" Sticker

Complete the official entry form and send to:
Pocket Books, GOFS Sweepstakes
1230 Avenue of the Americas, New York, NY 10020

Name_____(Child)

Birthdate_____/_____/_____

Name_____(Parent)

Address _____

City_____State_____Zip_____

Phone (_____)_____

See back for official rules   1302 (1 of 2)

POCKET BOOKS/"GOFS AUDIO" SWEEPSTAKES
Sweepstakes Official Rules:

1. No Purchase Necessary. Enter by mailing the completed Official Entry Form (no copies allowed) or by mailing a 3" x 5" card with your name and address to the Pocket Books/GOFS Sweepstakes,13th Floor, 1230 Avenue of the Americas, NY, NY 10020. Entries must be received by 6/30/97. Not responsible for lost, late, stolen, illegible, mutilated, incomplete, postage due or misdirected entries or mail or for typographical errors in the entry form or rules. Enter as often as you wish, but one entry per envelope. Winners will be selected at random from all eligible entries received in a drawing to be held on or about 7/1/97.

2. Prizes: One Grand Prize: A weekend (three day/two night) trip for up to four persons (the winning minor, one parent or legal guardian and two guests) including round-trip coach airfare from the major U.S. airport nearest the winner's residence to New York City, ground transportation or car rental in New York City, meals, two nights in a hotel (one room, occupancy for four) and lunch with R.L. Stine (approx. retail value $3500.000, trip must be taken on the date specified by Simon & Schuster, Inc.), Ten First Prizes: Walkman and Autographed "Ghosts of Fear Street" Audiobook (approx. retail value $40.00) Twenty Second Prizes: Autographed "Ghosts of Fear Street" T-shirt (approx. retail value $20.00 each), Thirty Third Prizes: Autographed "Ghosts of Fear Street" Audiobook (approx. retail value $7.95 each), Fifty Fourth Prizes: Autographed "Ghosts of Fear Street" Book (approx. retail value: $3.99) One Hundred Fifth Prizes: "Ghosts of Fear Street" Sticker (approx. retail value: $1.00)

3. The sweepstakes is open to residents of the U.S. and Canada, excluding Quebec, not older than fourteen as of 6/30/97. Proof of age required to claim prize. Prizes will be awarded to the winner's parent or legal guardian. Void in Puerto Rico and wherever prohibited or restricted by law. Simon & Schuster, Inc., Parachute Press, Inc., their respecitve officers, directors, shareholders, employees, suppliers, parents, subsidiaries, affiliates, agencies, sponsors, participating retailers, and persons connected with the use, marketing or conduct of this sweepstakes and their families living in the same household, are not eligible.

4. One prize per person or household. Prizes are not transferable and may not be substituted except by sponsor, in event of unavailability, in which case a prize of equal or greater value will be awarded. All prizes will be awarded. The odds of winning a prize depend upon the number of eligible entries received.

5. If a winner is a Canadian resident, then he/she must correctly answer a skill-based question administered by mail.

6. All expenses on receipt and use of prize including Federal, state and local taxes are the sole responsibility of the winners. Winners will be notified by mail. Winners may be required to execute and return an Affidavit of Eligibility and Release and all other legal documents which the sweepstakes sponsor may require (including a W-9 tax form) within 15 days of receipt of notification or an alternate winner will be selected.

7. Winners irrevocably grant Pocket Books, Parachute Press, Inc. and Simon & Schuster Audio the worldwide right, for no additional consideration, to use their names, photographs, likenesses, and entries for any advertising, promotion, marketing and publicity purposes relating to this promotional contest or otherwise without further compensation to or permission from the entrants, except where prohibited by law.

8. Winners agree that Simon & Schuster Inc., Parachute Press, Inc., their respective officers, directors, shareholders, employees, suppliers, parents, subsidiaries, affiliates, agencies, sponsors, participating retailers, and persons connected with the use, marketing or conduct of this sweepstakes, shall have no liability in connection with the collection, acceptance or use of the prizes awarded herein.

9. By participating in this sweepstakes, entrants agree to be bound by these rules and the decisions of the judges and sweepstakes sponsors, which are final in all matters relating to the sweepstakes.

10. For a list of major prize winners, (available after 7/11/97) send a stamped, self-addressed envelope to Prize Winners, Pocket Books/GOFS Sweepstakes, 13th Floor, 1230 Avenue of the Americas. NY, NY 10020.